Mommy's Coming Home from Treatment

Denise D. Crosson, Ph.D. • Illustrated by Mike Motz

CENTRAL RECOVERY PRESS

LAS VEGAS, NEVADA

Janey woke up all by herself. She grabbed her favorite doll and started
to dance around her room. Today is the day Mommy comes home!
Janey was so excited she couldn't stand still. When she tried to brush her teeth,
she got toothpaste all over the floor. When Daddy tried to comb her hair,
Janey wiggled so much Daddy dropped the comb.
When Janey ate her cereal, she spilled milk all over the table.
Finally, Daddy said, "Janey, you're just going to have to calm down."

Grandmom had been helping Janey and Daddy while Mommy was in treatment for her addiction. Mommy had been gone for five whole weeks. Janey loved her Grandmom, but she was ready to have Mommy home.

Janey wanted her Mommy to wake her up in the mornings again.
Janey wanted her Mommy to make her breakfast and sit with her while she ate.
Janey wanted her Mommy to pick her up after school and take her to the park.
Now the day to go get Mommy was finally here!

Before they went to get Mommy, they had to drop Grandmom off at the airport.
Janey was in such a hurry to get Mommy that she forgot to say good-bye
and hug her Grandmom. Grandmom's eyes started to fill with tears.
She said, "It hurts my feelings that after so many weeks of taking care of you,
you forgot to say good-bye."

Janey felt bad as soon as she realized she hurt Grandmom.
Janey said, "I'm sorry, Grandmom. Thank you for taking care of me.
I didn't mean to forget. I'm just in such a hurry to see Mommy."
Grandmom said that she understood and hugged Janey; but Janey
thought Grandmom still looked upset as she walked to the plane.
She didn't know what to do, so Janey didn't do anything.

Next, they had to make the long trip to the hospital.
Janey had been on the same trip once a week for the last five weeks,
and there was nothing new to see. Janey was bored with the farms and factories,
the spotted cows and brown horses, and the playful gray squirrels.
Janey asked her Daddy over and over, "How much longer until we get there?"

Daddy was patient for most of the trip until Janey asked the same question for what seemed like the hundredth time. Daddy said in a loud and stern voice, "Janey, you know exactly how long this trip takes. Please don't ask me again."

Now Janey was mad. Everybody was being grumpy today and she did not like it one bit. She didn't care that Mommy sometimes got angry or that Mommy did all those other scary things. Janey just wanted her Mommy NOW.

Finally, they arrived at Mommy's hospital. Janey unbuckled her seat belt
and jumped out of the car before Daddy got out. As she raced across the parking lot
toward the hospital entrance, Daddy yelled, "Janey! Stop right there, THIS INSTANT!"
Janey stopped in her tracks just as a car turned the corner
and drove right in front of her.

Daddy marched over to Janey and grabbed her by the hand.
He said, "Do you realize that car could've hit you?
You know better than to run without looking both ways when there are cars around.
I can't believe you did that." Janey hung her head and didn't move an inch.

Daddy walked so fast across the parking lot, Janey could barely keep up.
When they got inside the hospital, Mommy was waiting with all of her stuff piled
up around her. Mommy reached down and picked up Janey and gave her a great
big hug. Janey gave Mommy a kiss and said, "Let's go home, Mommy."

On the way home, Mommy and Daddy talked quietly.
Janey could not really hear them talking and she felt lonely
in the big empty back seat.

It was late afternoon by the time they pulled into the driveway.
Coming back home with Mommy was not nearly as exciting as Janey expected.
In fact, she felt sad and small and was afraid things would never feel right.

Janey slowly unbuckled her seat belt, climbed out of the car,
and walked toward the house. Daddy called out cheerfully,
"Hey, Janey, why don't you help us carry Mommy's stuff into the house?"
Janey turned around and pulled one of Mommy's smaller bags out of the trunk.

Janey carried the bag into the house, up the stairs, and into her parents' bedroom.
She dropped it on Mommy's bed, and then went to her room,
changed her clothes, and lay down. She didn't understand what had happened.
Mommy was home and she looked healthy, but things were still the same.

A little while later, Mommy came into Janey's room and sat on her bed
without saying anything at all. Janey wasn't sure what to think.
Mommy was never quiet like this before.

Finally Mommy asked, "Janey, how are you? You seem quiet and look sad today."
Janey thought a moment, then answered, "I was so excited about coming
to get you today that I ended up making everybody mad."

Mommy put her arm around Janey's shoulders. "Everybody's mad?" she asked.
"Who's everybody?" Janey sniffled and said, "Grandmom got mad at me
because I didn't say good-bye to her at the airport. Daddy got mad at me because
I asked too many questions, and then I ran out into the parking lot
without looking both ways."

"Oh." Mommy said. "I think I understand.
Remember how I would go to sleep and you couldn't wake me up? And how
sometimes I got angry with you, even though you didn't do anything wrong?
Well, I can't change those things I did, but I can do my very best
not to do them again. You can't change the things you did today that
made Daddy and Grandmom mad, but we can figure out a way to let
them know you are sorry and will try your best not to do them again."

"What do you think you can do to let Daddy and Grandmom know
that you are sorry about what happened today?"
Janey thought for a long time and said, "I could write Grandmom a thank-you card.
I could tell Daddy I'm sorry and that I'll be more careful around cars."

Mommy smiled and said, "Those are great ideas.
We could call Grandmom right now and thank her for her help.
What do you think?"

For the first time that day, Janey felt that things were going to be okay.
She said, "Okay, Mommy. I'll go talk with Daddy first, and then
we can call Grandmom together." Mommy smiled and said,
"That sounds like a good plan. I'll be downstairs when you're ready."

Janey went to look for Daddy. She looked in his bedroom, but it was empty.
She looked in the bathroom, but it was empty too. She looked in his office,
but it was dark and quiet. Janey went downstairs. Daddy wasn't in the living room.
He wasn't in the kitchen or the dining room either.

Finally, Janey found Daddy in the garage at his workbench. "Hi, Janey," he said. "Daddy I'm so sorry I made you mad today," Janey blurted. "I really wanted to hurry up and see Mommy. I'm sorry I asked you over and over again about getting to the hospital, and I know it was wrong to run into the parking lot without looking both ways."

"Honey, I was in a hurry to see Mommy, too. I'm sorry I wasn't very patient with you. I know I sounded grouchy when you ran into the parking lot, but I really was scared that you could've been hurt." Janey was so relieved Daddy was not mad at her that she started to cry.

Daddy knelt to hug Janey. "It's okay. Mommy's home and we're okay." Janey stopped crying and said, "I thought I was the only one who got scared. I didn't know you got scared, too." Daddy smiled and said, "Janey, everybody gets scared. We're just lucky we have each other. We can help out when one of us gets scared."

Daddy and Janey went to find Mommy. She was in the living room waiting for them. Together they called Grandmom. Janey talked to her first and said, "Grandmom, I'm sorry I was in such a hurry that I didn't say good-bye to you today. I love you and miss you already. Thank you for taking care of me." Grandmom thanked Janey for calling and said, "I loved taking care of you. I miss you, too."

After the phone call, Mommy started walking toward the door.
How strange, Janey thought. It was getting dark outside and Mommy almost
never left the house at night. The last time she did, Mommy wrecked the car.
Janey did not like the looks of this. Things were not the same
as before Mommy went to treatment, and yet they still felt strange.
Janey was tired and started to cry. "Where are you going?" she wailed.

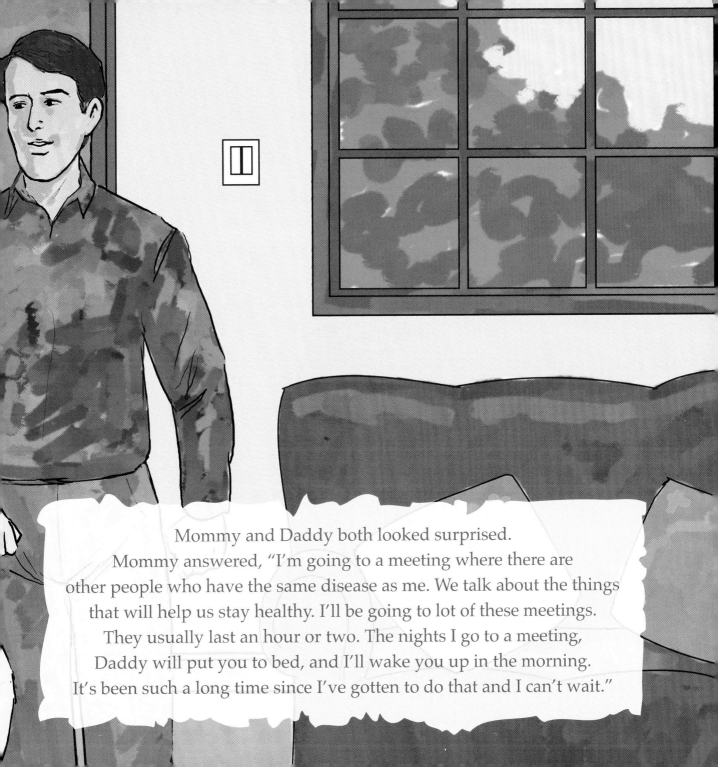

Mommy and Daddy both looked surprised.

Mommy answered, "I'm going to a meeting where there are other people who have the same disease as me. We talk about the things that will help us stay healthy. I'll be going to lot of these meetings. They usually last an hour or two. The nights I go to a meeting, Daddy will put you to bed, and I'll wake you up in the morning. It's been such a long time since I've gotten to do that and I can't wait."

Mommy kissed Janey, picked up her purse, and walked out of the door. Janey continued to cry. Daddy put his arm around Janey and said, "Hey, I know it's been a long day, and I can see you're worn out. Let's get you ready for bed."

As Daddy tucked Janey into bed, he said, "Janey, I love you. Sleep tight.
Mommy will wake you up in the morning."
Janey sniffled and hugged her favorite doll as she drifted off to sleep.

In the morning when Janey opened her eyes, the first thing she saw
was her Mommy's smile. Janey sat up and hugged her Mommy tightly.
Today was going to be a good day.

The End

Talking with Children about Addiction Treatment
A Guide for Parents

1. **Focus on the positive.** Anytime it's necessary to explain a difficult situation to a child, such as when a parent starts addiction treatment, try to balance happy times with times not so happy. This helps teach that in the best of times there are things that are not perfect and in difficult times there are things worth celebrating.

2. **Keep it simple—at a child's level.** When talking with more than one child, speak at the youngest level. Once everyone understands the basics, encourage questions. If there is a large age difference, talk to everyone first and then follow up individually.

3. **Be completely honest.** Start with something like, "Mommy's gone to the hospital to get help for her drug use." Watch and listen to the child's response and answer any questions.

4. **Initiate the conversation;** do not wait for the child to ask about where the parent is or what has and will be happening. Putting off this important discussion only increases the child's sense of uncertainty and worry.

5. **Do not lecture.** Do not talk at or down to the child. Don't assume this is too complex a topic for children. Don't tell the child about what he or she should feel or believe. Ask about feelings, and then listen carefully to the answers. You want to present a calm presence so the child will feel safe to share whatever emotions he or she is experiencing.

6. **Be helpful; try to understand the concerns, feelings, and beliefs of the child.** Once you understand, offer help and support. This might sound like, "You've told me you are feeling _____. When I feel _____ it helps me if the people I love do _____. Would that be something you'd like? Is there something I can do that would work better for you?" Remember, all children need reassurance. Younger children often only need basic information and consistent reassurance that they are not to blame and that the absent parent loves them and will be back.

7. **Share your own feelings and concerns.** It's important to give a simple honest disclosure of your emotional state, but it should be framed positively and reassuringly. For example: "With Daddy gone for several weeks, I sometimes feel sad. Fortunately, Grandma is helping us out and that makes things easier for me. All of your help has really meant a lot to me, too. I'm sorry if I was grumpy this morning. I don't want to take out feeling sad on you." Remember to not make the child your confidant.

8. **Share your values,** including that people we love are loveable even when they disappoint or inconvenience us. Communicate that addiction and mental illness are diseases like diabetes and high blood pressure that need treatment and support.

9. **Be available;** do not make the "crisis" the entire focus of your lives. While you may need to eliminate some family activities, keep those important for your own self-care and support. You cannot support others or your children without first taking care of your own needs.

10. **Be patient and supportive.** It is common for children under stress to be extra needy and fall back on behavior they grew out of months before. If the behavior goes on too long or seems beyond your ability, talk with your child's primary health care provider.

11. **Be clear and specific about everything,** including that you are available and want your children to talk about feelings, questions, or worries at any time. It is important you are consistent and reassuring. If you are overwhelmed and worried, settle yourself and get the support you need before starting the conversation with your child.

Important Talking Points to Remember

Neither the child nor others in the family caused the problem.

* * *

Neither the child nor others in the family can control the disease.

* * *

Neither the child nor others in the family are able to cure the disease, but treatment is effective and the parent/family member is receiving treatment.

The most important thing the child and other family members can do is take good care of themselves.

* * *

Taking good care of yourself always includes communicating feelings, making healthy choices, and celebrating who you are—specifically your strengths and abilities—as an individual and as a family.

ABOUT THE AUTHOR

Denise D. Crosson, Ph.D. has been a nurse for twenty-five years, a nurse practitioner for nine years, and a nurse researcher for five years. Her first job working with children was in high school as a lifeguard and swim instructor at the YMCA. Throughout her nursing career, Crosson has worked with children and their families in hospital, home, hospice, and community-based settings. She earned a masters and doctoral degree from Virginia Commonwealth University where she was a fellow in the VA-LEND neurodevelopmental disabilities training program, which focused on children and families. Her dissertation research focused on short- and long-term effects of preterm birth on childhood development.

Crosson lives in Las Vegas, Nevada. This is her second book for children.

ABOUT THE ILLUSTRATOR

Mike Motz is an award-winning illustrator from Canada who has illustrated twenty-five children's books.

CENTRAL RECOVERY PRESS

Central Recovery Press (CRP) is committed to publishing exceptional material addressing addiction treatment and recovery, including original and quality books, audio/visual communications, and web-based new media. Through a diverse selection of titles, it seeks to impact the behavioral healthcare field with a broad range of unique resources for professionals, recovering individuals, and their families. For more information, visit www.centralrecoverypress.com.

CRP donates a portion of its proceeds to the *Foundation for Recovery,* a nonprofit organization local and national in scope. Its purpose is to promote recovery from addiction through a variety of forums, such as direct services, research and development, education, study of recovery alternatives, public awareness, and advocacy.

Central Recovery Press, Las Vegas, 89129
© 2009 by Central Recovery Press, Las Vegas, NV

ISBN-13: 978-0-9799869-4-9
ISBN-10: 0-9799869-4-X

Publisher: Central Recovery Press
            3371 N Buffalo Drive
            Las Vegas, NV 89129

Typeset by Sara Streifel, Think Creative Design

CENTRAL RECOVERY PRESS
LAS VEGAS, NEVADA